WHO IS THE KING

Written by
**Leah Chana
Rubabshi**

Illustrated by
**Yael
Pushkin**

A Midrashic Tale on the

POWER
OF THE
TONGUE

FELDHEIM PUBLISHERS
JERUSALEM · NEW YORK

In memory of my beloved grandparents
David and Rose Levy

ISBN 978-1-68025-267-5

Edited by Sherie Gross

FELDHEIM PUBLISHERS
POB 43163, Jerusalem, Israel

208 Airport Executive Park
Nanuet, NY 10954
www.feldheim.com

Distributed in Europe by:
LEHMANNS
+44–0–191–430–0333
info@lehmanns.co.uk
www.lehmanns.co.uk

Distributed in Australia by:
GOLDS WORLD OF JUDAICA
+613 95278775
info@golds.com.au
www.golds.com.au

Printed in Israel

The royal King of Persia was suddenly sick.
He needed some help and some medicine, quick!
They called in the doctors to find him a cure,
and thought that the king would get better, for sure.

But nothing was helping, the pain only grew.
Then one doctor said he knew just what to do.
"I know how to cure him, now don't get upset.
He needs lion's milk, which is quite hard to get."

"I'm happy to help," cried a man from the crowd.
"Just give me ten goats," said the man as he bowed.

He went to the jungle, so far, far away,
and found a few lions the very first day.

A lioness saw him and stood on her feet.
He sent her a goat to have something to eat.

The next day he came
to the very same spot.
He sent her a goat,
and much closer he got.

He kept sending goats
till she seemed very near,
and soon she approached him
without any fear.

While milking a lioness
seemed quite bizarre,
he managed to put
all the milk in a jar.

He then had a vision that very same night
that parts of his body all started to fight.

His **legs** said to all,
"No one else can compare
to legs that can walk, and took all of us there."

"But **hands** grabbed the milk,
and we're sure as can be
that **we** get the thanks;
yes, we know you'll agree."

His **heart** started racing
and beating so strong,
"It's due to my courage,
you're all very wrong."

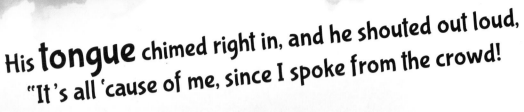

His **tongue** chimed right in, and he shouted out loud,
"It's all 'cause of me, since I spoke from the crowd!

The tongue is the ruler
of all body parts,
of hands and of legs
and of fast-beating hearts."

His limbs disagreed,

his heartbeat went faster,

"I'll prove to you all...

...that the tongue is the master!"

The man soon returned
to the king on his bed,
and handed the doctor
the milk as he said,

"I traveled the jungle
and went very far
to bring you **dog's milk**,
which I put in this jar."

The king was enraged,
"For your words, you will die!"
They took him to jail,
as he started to cry.

The king told his guards
that the man should be hung.

His limbs shook with fear
and they yelled at the tongue,

"The tongue is the ruler, and if you'll agree,
I'll take back my words to erase the decree."

"Oh yes, we agree! You're the king, it's so true!
There's nobody here more important than you!"

The tongue called the guard
to come quick, right away.
"I must see the king,
I have something to say!"

"Your Honor, I beg you, I must not be hung!
The words that I spoke were a slip of the tongue.
I brought lion's milk, it's as pure as can be.
Please drink from the cup, and a cure you will see."

The king heard his words
and he felt reassured.
He took a big sip
and was instantly cured!

He let the man go,
all his limbs screamed "Hooray!"
And they all learned the lesson
to watch what we say.

מות וחיים ביד לשון

Death
and life
are in
the power
of the
tongue.

(Mishlei 18:21)